W9-CNO-679

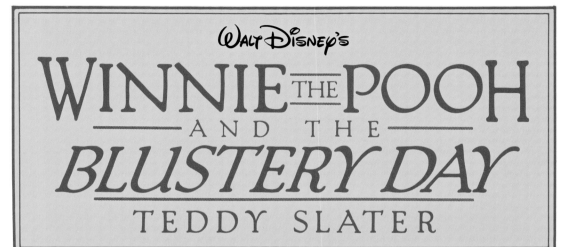

Walt Disney's

WINNIE THE POOH
AND THE
BLUSTERY DAY

TEDDY SLATER

ILLUSTRATED BY

BILL LANGLEY AND DIANA WAKEMAN

Disney
PRESS

NEW YORK

''A Rather Blustery Day''
Words and Music by
Richard M. Sherman and Robert B. Sherman.
Copyright © 1964 Wonderland Music Company, Inc.
Copyright Renewed.
Used by Permission. All Rights Reserved.

''The Wonderful Thing About Tiggers''
Words and Music by
Richard M. Sherman and Robert B. Sherman.
Copyright © 1964 Wonderland Music Company, Inc.
Copyright Renewed.
Used by Permission. All Rights Reserved.

Based on the Pooh stories by A. A. Milne
(copyright The Pooh Properties Trust).

Library of Congress Catalog Card Number: 92-55130
ISBN 1-56282-488-0

Walt Disney's

WINNIE THE POOH
AND THE
BLUSTERY DAY

One fine day, the East wind traded places with the West wind, and that stirred things up a bit in the Hundred-Acre Wood.

And on that windy day, Winnie the Pooh decided to visit his Thoughtful Spot. As he walked along, he made up a little hum. This is how it went:

Oh, the wind is lashing lustily,
and the trees are thrashing thrustily,
and the leaves are rustling gustily,
so it feels that it will undoubtedly be . . .
a rather blustery day!

As soon as Pooh reached his Thoughtful Spot, he sat right down and tried to think of something.

"Think, think, think, think, think," Pooh mumbled to himself. But nothing came to mind.

"Think, think, think," Pooh tried again, putting one paw to his head as if to catch any stray thoughts that might come wandering along.

Suddenly Gopher popped out of his gopher hole and said, "What's wrong, sonny? Got yourself a headache?"

"No," Pooh replied. "I was just thinking."

"Is that so?" said Gopher. "Well, if I were you, I'd think about skedaddling out of here. It's Windsday, you know."

"Windsday? Why, so it is," said Pooh. And then he finally had a thought—and it was a good one, at that. "I think I shall go wish everyone a happy Windsday," Pooh announced. "And I shall begin with my very dear friend Piglet."

Piglet lived in the middle of the forest in a very grand house. And on this blustery day, he was sweeping the fallen leaves away from his front door. He had just swept the last leaf away when a big gust of wind blew it right back at him, scooping him up and whisking him away. "I don't mind the leaves that are leaving . . . ," Piglet observed. "It's the leaves that are coming." And with that, he was blown right into Pooh Bear.

"Happy Windsday," said Pooh as another great gust of wind lifted Piglet right off his little pink feet.

"Well, it isn't very happy for me," Piglet said with a gulp.

"Where are you going?" Pooh cried, running after his friend.

"That's what I'm asking myself," Piglet said. "Where . . . ?"

"And what do you think you will answer yourself?" Pooh asked, grabbing hold of Piglet's scarf just before he floated out of reach.

"Oh, Pooh, I'm unraveling!" Piglet cried.

Indeed he was. Or rather, his scarf was. Like a pink kite on a long green string, Piglet went sailing off into the sky.

"Oh dear. Oh d-d-d-dear, dear," he stammered, clutching onto the string.

"Hang on, Piglet," cried Pooh from down below.

It wasn't long before Piglet was flying over Kanga's house. Kanga had just hopped outside to get the mail.

"Look, Mama," said Roo, peering out of his mother's pouch. "A kite!"

"That's not a kite," said Kanga. "It's Piglet!"

And before Kanga could say another word, Pooh skidded to a stop in front of her. "Happy Windsday, Kanga," he said. "Happy Windsday, Roo."

"Can I fly Piglet next, Pooh?" Roo asked.

But Pooh and Piglet had already breezed past little Roo.

"Oh dear, oh dear, oh-dear-oh-dear-oh-dear," cried Piglet as he swooped right and left in the gusty air.

"Oh bo-bo-bother," Pooh exclaimed, bouncing and sliding along below him.

When Piglet finally found the nerve to look down, there was Eeyore, looking up at him. Eeyore was busy repairing his house, which the wind had blown to pieces. He had just put the last stick back in place when Pooh came crashing through.

"Happy Windsday, Eeyore," said Pooh. Then he went zipping off again, still holding on to the remains of Piglet's scarf.

"Thanks for noticin' me," said Eeyore.

Not far from Eeyore's house was Rabbit's garden.

"Ah, what a refreshing day for harvesting," Rabbit said aloud as he pulled up a large orange carrot.

Looking up, he suddenly saw Pooh coming toward him at top speed.

"Oh no!" shouted Rabbit, waving his arms frantically.

"Happy Windsday," Pooh called, kicking up a whole row of carrots.

"Oh *yes*!" Rabbit chuckled as the juicy, ripe carrots fell smack into his wheelbarrow. "Next time I hope he plows right through my rutabaga patch."

Stronger and stronger the West wind blew. And before long, Piglet found himself blown right up against Owl's window.

Owl was awakened from a peaceful snooze by the loud crash. "Whoo?" he said, opening his big round eyes. "Who is it?"

"It's me," Piglet said. "P-p-p-please, may I come in?"

"Well, I say now," Owl said, his eyes rounder than ever. "Someone has pasted Piglet on my window."

Just then Pooh's face appeared beside Piglet's, and Owl invited them both in. Soon Pooh and Piglet were comfortably seated in Owl's cozy living room. "Am I correct in assuming that it's a rather blustery day?" asked Owl.

"Oh, yes. That reminds me. Happy Windsday, Owl," said Pooh, hungrily eyeing a big honeypot in front of him on the table.

"Windsday?" Owl hooted as the wind whistled through his house. "My good fellow, I wouldn't go so far as to call it Windsday. Just a mild zephyr."

"Excuse me, Owl, but is there any honey in that pot?" Pooh shouted over the howling wind.

"Oh, yes, of course," Owl said. "Help yourself." While Pooh eagerly reached for the pot of honey—which the wind had just blown clear across the table—Owl continued with his story.

"As I was saying, this is just a mild zephyr compared to the big wind of sixty-seven. Or was it seventy-six?" Owl muttered, scratching his head. "Oh well, no matter. I remember the big blow well. It was the year my aunt Clara went to visit her cousin. Now, her cousin was not only gifted on the glockenspiel, but . . ."

And with the wild wind roaring through his house, Owl proceeded to tell his friends all about his aunt Clara's cousin. He didn't seem to notice when the teacups clattered to the floor. And he barely paused when the wind swept Piglet right out the door and back in again. It wasn't until the whole house came crashing down upon his ears that Owl finally finished his tale.

As soon as Christopher Robin heard the news, he hurried to the scene of Owl's disaster.

"What a pity," said Christopher Robin when he saw the state Owl's house was in. "I don't think we will ever be able to fix it."

"If you ask me," said Eeyore, "when a house looks like that, it's time to find another one." Then he shook his head and said, "It might take a day or two, but don't worry, Owl—I'll find you a new one."

"Good," said Owl, settling back in his rocking chair. "That will just give me time to tell you about my uncle Clyde. . . ."

And that's just what he did. On and on Owl talked until the blustery day turned into a blustery night.

For Pooh it turned out to be an anxious sort of night, filled with anxious sorts of noises. One was a particular noise he'd never heard before:

"*Rrrrrrr!*"

It wasn't a rumble. It wasn't a grumble. And it wasn't exactly a growl. But whatever it was, it was coming from just outside Pooh's door.

"Is that you, Piglet?" Pooh called, but no one answered. "Eeyore?" Pooh tried again. And finally, "Christopher Robin?"

When there was still no answer, Pooh got out of bed and went to investigate. And being a bear of very little brain, he decided to invite the new sound in.

"Hello?" he said, flinging the front door open.

Suddenly a big, bouncy creature bounded in and knocked Pooh flat on his back.

"*Rrrrrr.* Hello," the creature said from atop Pooh's chest. "I'm Tigger."

"Oh," Pooh replied, looking up into Tigger's smiling face. "You scared me."

"Sure I did," Tigger said good-naturedly. "Everyone's scared of Tiggers. Who are you?"

"I'm Pooh," said Pooh.

"Ah, what's a Pooh?" Tigger asked.

"You're sitting on one," Pooh informed him.

And with no further ado, Tigger climbed off Pooh, stuck out his paw, and said, "Glad to meet ya. Tigger's my name. T-I—double Guh—Er. That spells Tigger!"

"But what's a Tigger?" Pooh asked, plainly puzzled.

Without a pause, Tigger proudly replied:

The wonderful thing about Tiggers
   is Tiggers are wonderful things.
Their tops are made out of rubber,
   and their bottoms are made of springs.
They're bouncy, trouncy, flouncy, pouncy,
   fun, fun, fun, fun, fun.
But the most wonderful thing about Tiggers
   is that I'm the only one!

And to prove his point, Tigger bounced around the room on his springy tail repeating: "I'm the only one!"

"If you're the only one, what's that over there?" Pooh asked, pointing at Tigger's reflection in the mirror.

"What a strange-looking creature!" said Tigger. "Look at the beady little eyes, pur-posti-rus chin, and ricky-diculus striped pajamas!"

Pooh nodded, and then he said, "Looks like another Tigger to me."

Tigger decided to change the subject. "Ah, well, did I say I was hungry?"

"I don't think so," said Pooh.

"Well, then, I'll say it," said Tigger. "I'm hungry."

"Not for honey, I hope," Pooh said, casting a worried glance at his honeypot.

"Oh boy, honey!" Tigger cried. "That's what Tiggers like best."

"I was afraid of that," Pooh said as Tigger plopped down at the table, grabbed the honey, and dug his paw in.

"Yum," Tigger said, putting a glob of honey in his mouth. "*Yuck!*" he said when he swallowed his first mouthful.

"Tiggers *don't* like honey," he gagged. "That sticky stuff is only fit for heffalumps and woozles."

"You mean elephants and weasels," Pooh corrected him.

"That's what I said. Heffalumps and woozles," Tigger said.

"Well, what do heff . . . ah . . . ah . . . hallalaff, ah . . . what do they do?" Pooh inquired.

"Oh, nothin' much," Tigger said nonchalantly. "Just steal honey." And with that, he went bouncing out the door and into the night.

Suddenly Pooh was all alone. . . . Or was he?

Pooh had a horrible feeling that at least one heffalump—or was it a woozle?—was lurking about outside. So he bolted the door and picked up his pop gun, determined to stand guard over his honey.

Hour after hour, Pooh kept his lonely vigil while the very blustery night turned into a very rainy night. Lightning flashed. Thunder crashed. And somewhere between the flashing and crashing, Pooh fell asleep.

Pooh dreamed he was surrounded by heffalumps and woozles of all shapes and sizes. Some were black, and some were brown. Some were up, and some were down. Some had polka dots. Some had stripes. But they all had one thing in common: THEY ALL WANTED TO STEAL HIS HONEY!

As Pooh tightly clutched his honeypot, one of the heffalumps turned into a watering can and began dousing him with water. The chilly drops cascaded over Pooh, soaking him from head to toe.

He woke up suddenly, and the heffalumps and woozles were gone. But the water remained. It was already up to Pooh's knees, and more was leaking in through the ceiling.

Pooh slogged across the flooded floor to his mirror. After studying the very damp bear reflected there, he asked, "Is it raining where you are?" And without even waiting for an answer, he said, "It's raining where I am, too."

As a matter of fact, it was raining all over the Hundred-Acre Wood. The rain came down, down, down, and the river rose up, up, up, rising so high it finally crept out of its bed and into Piglet's.

Poor Piglet was terrified. With the water swirling around him, he grabbed paper and pen and frantically scribbled: ''HELP! P . . . P . . . PIGLET. (ME.)'' Then he placed the message in a bottle and tossed it out his window and into the raging river.

As the rain came down, Piglet tried to scoop it up into a big iron pot. But the pot was not—most definitely not!—big enough for all that water.

Floating atop a wooden chair, Piglet kept on bailing, but as he was bailing, he went sailing through the door.

Meanwhile, Pooh was having quite a difficult time himself. He had managed to save ten honeypots, and he sat with them on the branch of a tree, high above the river. More than ready for his supper, he stuck his head into one of the pots. But as Pooh tried to sop up his supper, the river sopped up Pooh, for he fell off the branch and into the swirling water below. Upside down, with his head still stuck in the honey-pot, Pooh was carried along with the current.

The Hundred-Acre Wood got floodier and floodier. But the water couldn't come all the way up to Christopher Robin's house, so that's where everyone gathered. Everyone except Piglet, Pooh, and Eeyore, that is.

In the midst of all the excitement, Eeyore stubbornly stuck to his task of finding a new home for Owl.

While Eeyore was off house hunting, Roo made an important discovery. "Look!" he said. "I've found a bottle, and it's got something in it, too."

"It's a message," Christopher Robin declared. "It says: 'Help! P . . . P . . . Piglet. (Me.)' "

Turning to Owl, he said, "You must fly over to Piglet's house and tell him we'll make a rescue."

So Owl flew out over the flood, and soon he spotted two small objects below him.

One was little Piglet, caught in a whirlpool. And the other was Pooh, floating downstream, his head still stuck in the honeypot.

"Oh, Owl," Piglet said. "I don't mean to c-c-complain, but I'm so s-s-scared."

"Be brave, little Piglet," Owl advised. "Chin up and all that sort of thing."

"It's awfully hard to be b-b-brave when you're such a s-s-small animal," Piglet pointed out.

"Then to divert your small mind from your unfortunate predicament, I shall tell you an amusing anecdote," Owl offered. "It concerns a distant cousin of mine. . . ."

Owl had just begun his story when Piglet cried, "I beg your pardon, Owl, but I think we're coming to a flutterfall, a falatterfall, a very big w-waterfall!"

"Please," said Owl, holding up a warning wing. "No interruptions."

But Piglet was already being carried away by the current. A moment later he fell over the falls, with Pooh Bear close behind.

Head over heels the two friends tumbled down the rushing, gushing waterfall—down, down, down until they finally landed in a quiet pool far, far, far below.

"Oh, there you are, Pooh Bear," Owl said as Pooh popped up on Piglet's chair. "Now, to continue my story. . . ."

Fortunately for Pooh, Owl didn't have time to finish his story, for they quickly floated to the river's edge, where Christopher Robin and the others were waiting.

"Pooh!" Christopher Robin cried, lifting him off the chair. "Thank goodness you're safe. But where is Piglet?"

All of a sudden something emerged from under the chair. It was Pooh's honeypot!

"H-h-here I am," Piglet replied from inside the pot.

"Pooh!" Christopher Robin cried again. "You rescued Piglet."

"I did?" Pooh said.

"Yes," Christopher Robin said, patting Pooh on the head. "And it was a very brave thing to do. You are a hero!"

"I am?" Pooh said.

"Yes," Christopher Robin said. "And as soon as the flood is over, I shall give you a hero party."

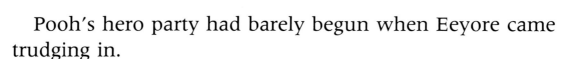

Pooh's hero party had barely begun when Eeyore came trudging in.

"I found a house for Owl," he said.

"I say, Eeyore, good show!" Owl hooted happily. "Where, may I ask, is it?"

"Follow me, and I'll show you," Eeyore said.

So everyone followed Eeyore. But much to their surprise, when they got to Owl's new house, it turned out to be . . .

. . . Piglet's house!

"Why are we stopping here?" Christopher Robin asked.

"This is Owl's new house," Eeyore said proudly. "What do you think of it?"

There was a long moment of silence. Then Christopher Robin said, "It's a nice house, Eeyore, but . . ."

And Kanga said, "It's a lovely house, but . . ."

"It's the best house in the whole world," Piglet sighed, his eyes full of tears.

"Tell them it's your house, Piglet," Pooh whispered.

But Piglet didn't have the heart to disappoint Owl. "No,"
he said. "This house belongs—*sniff*—to our good friend Owl."

"But Piglet," Rabbit said, "where will *you* live?"

"Well . . . ," Piglet said. "I-I-I guess—*sniff*—I shall l-live—"

"With me," Pooh broke in, taking Piglet's hand in his.
"You shall live with me, won't you, Piglet?"

"With you?" Piglet said, wiping a tear from his eye. "Oh,
thank you, Pooh Bear. Of course I will."

"Piglet, that was a very grand thing to do," Christopher Robin said, taking Piglet's other hand.

"A heroic thing," Rabbit chimed in.

And that's when Pooh had his second good thought in two days. "Christopher Robin," he asked, "can we make a one-hero party into a two-hero party?"

"Of course we can, silly old bear," said Christopher Robin. And so they did.

Pooh was a hero for saving Piglet, and Piglet was a hero for giving Owl his grand home in the beech tree.

To celebrate these deeds of bravery and generosity, everyone gathered round the heroes, shouting, "Hip, hip, hooray for the Piglet and the Pooh."

Then Pooh and Piglet were scooped up in a blanket and tossed high, high, high into the clear blue sky.